Jack and Jill went up the hill

Dickery, dickery, dare,
The Pig flew up in the air

I saw a ship
a-sailing

Hush-a-bye, baby, on the tree-top

Baa, baa,
black sheep

Rain, rain
go away

Hark! hark!
the dogs bark

Ding, dong, bell
The cat is in the
well!

Ring a-round a rosie,
a pocket full of posie

Twinkle, twinkle, little star